14 DAY

TL-BML-054

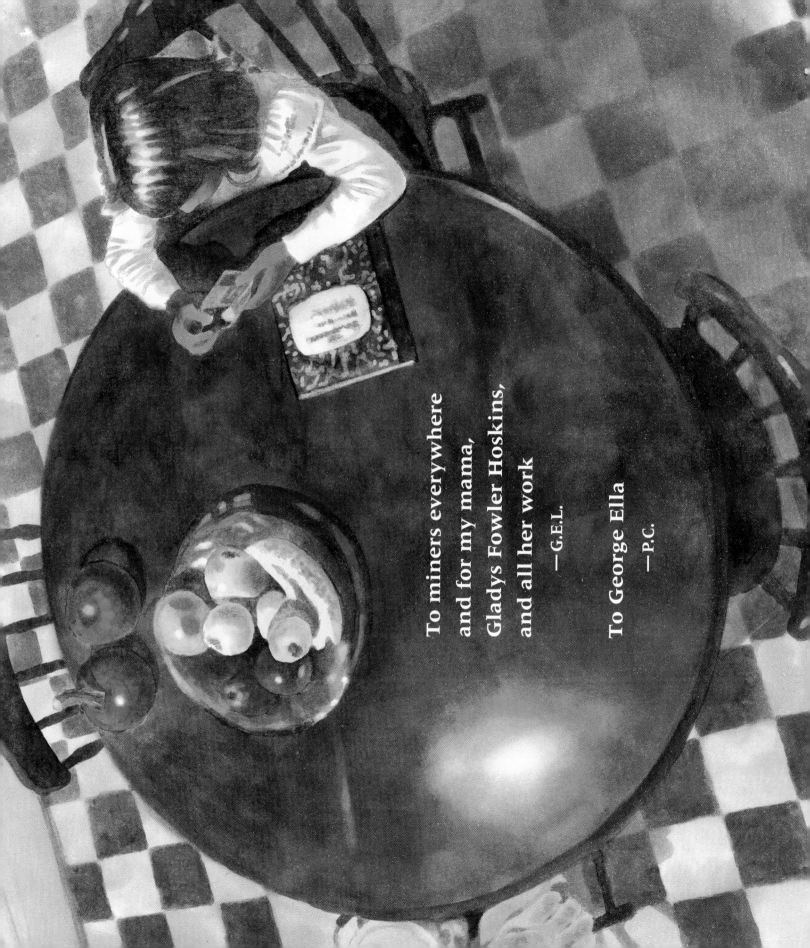

To miners everywhere
and for my mama,
Gladys Fowler Hoskins,
and all her work
—G.E.L.

To George Ella
—P.C.

Mama is a Miner

story by GEORGE ELLA LYON

paintings by PETER CATALANOTTO

ORCHARD BOOKS • New York

Special thanks to Marat Moore, writer, former miner, and historian of women miners, for technical consultation; the United Mine Workers of America photographic archives; Paul Pratt, Mike Coldiron, James B. Coomes, Jr., Daven Hoskins, and New Horizons Coal (Harlan County, Kentucky) for the guided tour of Dulcimer #7—G.E.L.

In memory of my ancestors, the Bunches, who mined the coal from the Appalachian Mountains

Special thanks to Gladys Hoskins, the Kingsbauer family, Jessie, Ms. Ellis's first graders, Jo-Ann for her eye, and, as always, DJ for his trust—P.C.

Orchard Books, 95 Madison Avenue, New York, NY 10016

Manufactured in the United States of America. Printed by Barton Press, Inc. Bound by Horowitz/Rae. Title page typography by Marjika Kostiw. The text of this book is set in 18 point Meridien Bold condensed. The illustrations are watercolor paintings reproduced in full color.

10 9 8 7 6 5 4 3 2 1

Library of Congress Cataloging-in-Publication Data. Lyon, George Ella, date. Mama is a miner / story by George Ella Lyon; paintings by Peter Catalanotto.   p.   cm. "A Richard Jackson book" —Half t.p. Summary: A daughter describes her mother's job working as a miner. ISBN 0-531-06853-6.   ISBN 0-531-08703-4 (lib. bdg.) [1. Mothers—Fiction.   2. Miners—Fiction.   3. Work—Fiction.   4. Stories in rhyme.] I. Catalanotto, Peter, ill.   II. Title.   PZ8.L9893Mam   1994   [E]—dc20   93-49398

Mama is a miner.

She rides the mantrip in.

When I'm settled on Bus 34
Mama's crowded into a low car
cap light off, dozing, swaying
headed for Black Mountain's heart.

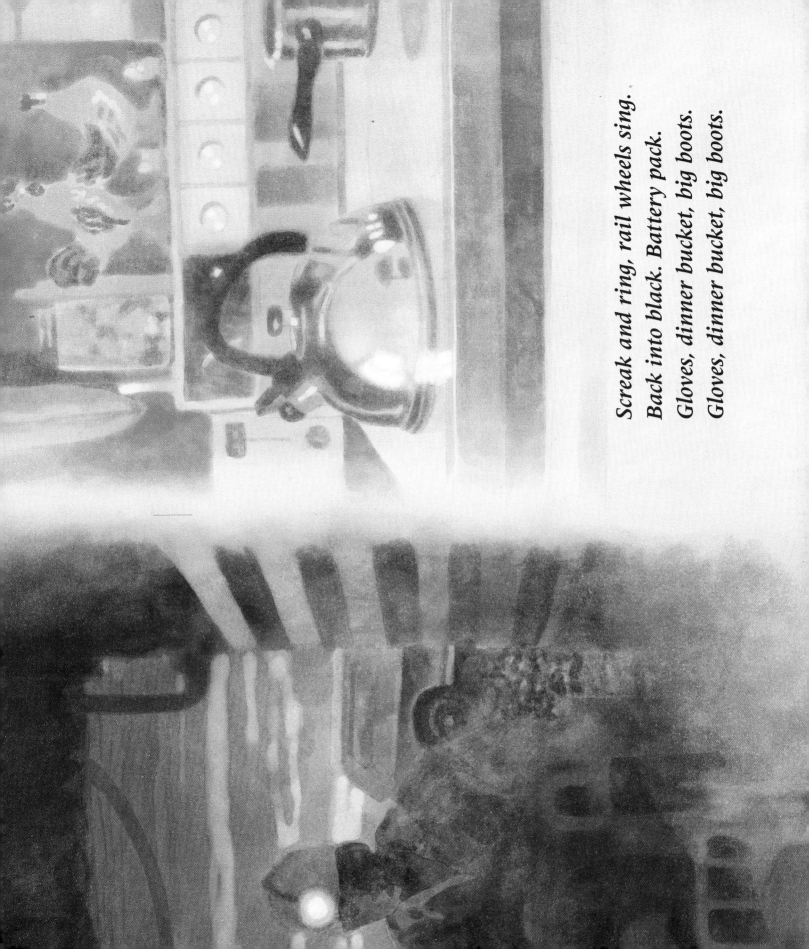

Screak and ring, rail wheels sing.
Back into black. Battery pack.
Gloves, dinner bucket, big boots.
Gloves, dinner bucket, big boots.

When the mantrip stops
two miles in
Mama climbs out
at Linefork Mains
with Nikko and Eldon,
Arlene and Dave,
her crew at Lynch Number 8.

Some days they're sent to the working face
to watch the roof or keep cable clear
while the continuous miner
roars at the rock
and rips coal from the seam.

They spread rock dust
on the roof and ribs,
wet the face so there'll be no spark
to explode trapped gas or floating dust.
"Safety first," Mama says.

Firedamp, blackdamp,
Fire Boss checks the air.
Bad top, kettle bottom:
don't go there.

Just last month, Eldon's leg got hurt.
I wish Mama still worked at the store
away from explosions, roof fall, dark.
But ringing up grub didn't pay our bills.
"Hard work for hard times," Mama says.

Some days she's a shoveler,
scooping up coal spilled from the belt
that moves it up to the mouth of the mine.

She bends and sweats with Nikko and Dave
while mud sucks at their rubber boots
and their cap lights bob in the glittery dark
like underground lightning bugs.

*Son of a quarter
daughter of a dime,
shoveling soup
on the old belt line.*

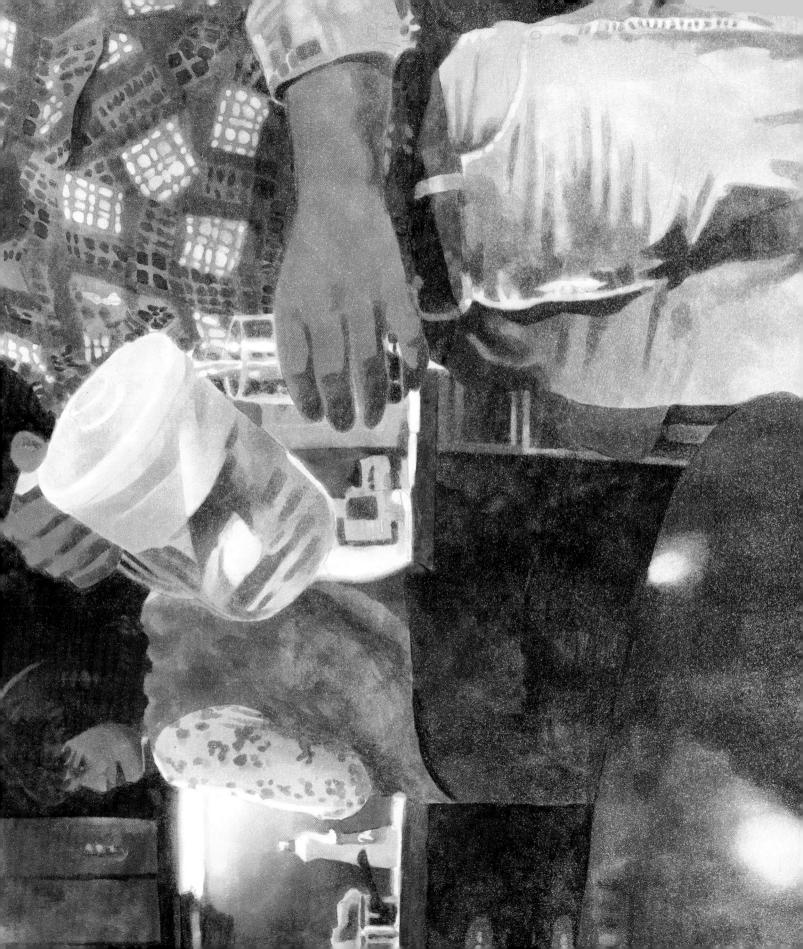

"First half of the shift," Mama says,
"I tell myself I'm digging for lunch,
for time to sit in the dinner hole
with Eldon and the rest of the crew,
eating ham sandwiches just like you
back on top of the earth."

Forgot to set a rock
on your dinner bucket?
Tail raised the lid,
rat teeth took it.

"What about second half?" I ask.
"Second half's better," Mama says,
serving up beans, cutting corn bread.
"Then I'm digging for home."

Dig and scrape, dinner on a plate.
Lift and load, coal truck on the road.
Mountain gold, black as night.
Some big city's heat and light.

Sometimes in gym or reading or math
a door will creak, a chair will grate
and I pretend it's Mama I hear—

Mama miles deep
in the cap-lit tunnel
digging

digging for home.